The Earth Visitor
and Alexia

Esther R. Smith

Kindle Direct Publishing

ISBN: 9798344485652

Printed in the United States of America

CHAPTER ONE

"Where are you, Sis?" shouted Chris. Twenty-two-year-old Chris and twenty-year-old Sarah were siblings who lived together in the family home following the death of their parents.

"I'm here in my closet, but just a minute, and I'll meet you in the living room," Sarah replied. Once she was facing him, she asked, "What do you want?"

"I just got a message on my phone. My friends are going to arrive here in about fifteen minutes. I was about ready to walk the three blocks to Pete's house while his parents were gone visiting his grandparents. For some reason, Pete said on the phone just now, his parents came home early and now our group can't meet there today. He wondered if they could come here instead. I said that would be okay. He is phoning our group about the change in plans. Sis, this would not be a good place for you to be with my friends if they become intoxicated during this New Year's Eve celebration."

"You're right, Chris. I'll get ready to leave right away. I can stay with Grandma tonight. Tomorrow morning at nine o'clock, I'm scheduled to babysit for friends of mine. I probably won't get back home until after supper tomorrow."

"Gee, Sarah, that should all work out great. Give me your keys so I can park your car in the driveway. Then, you'll be able to leave quickly once you pack your suitcase. I'll put my bag of glazed donuts on your car's front seat. I know these are the kind that Grandma especially likes. I was going to take them to Pete's house, but that isn't going to happen now. Those coming here will each bring some food or a drink with them. Instead of donuts, I'll place your home baked cookies in a bowl. My buddies will really like those.

Have a good time, Sis, with Grandma. I know she'll be glad to see you."

As Sarah started to drive away from the house, a blue car stopped at the curb to allow her to exit the driveway. After her car moved onto the paved street, the blue car drove into the driveway. Sarah saw that in her car's rearview mirror and smiled. Obviously, she had managed to leave just in time.

She knew the route to Grandma's house. She was a frequent visitor there. Actually, Sarah decided, it was going to be nice spending New Year's Eve with Grandma who lived alone and who would appreciate having company this particular night. Sarah had previously decided to stay off the streets this evening to avoid the likelihood of meeting a car with a drunk driver celebrating the coming New Year.

Grandma greeted her favorite grandchild warmly when Sarah rang the doorbell. They chatted for a few minutes, and then Grandma said, "I was thinking of you, honey. I was wondering if you'd like the notes I've saved over the years regarding my contacts with alien visitors to Earth. When I had several things to remember about them, I started jotting down notes and placing those in individual envelopes with the year and subject on the outside. I eventually thought about writing a book. I'd title it *The Earth Visitor*. I just never got around to writing it. I'm hoping maybe you will help me do it. Here, sit at the kitchen table while I go get the box with the notes. We can read them here at the table."

Grandma took only three steps when the buzzer sounded indicating a visitor at the back door. Grandma smiled. She pushed a red button near the kitchen light switch. The buzzing sound stopped. Then the back porch door opened. A tall man in his early twenties came into the kitchen. Sarah stood politely to meet the newcomer.

The newcomer smiled at Sarah when he noticed her. Grandma said, "Tom, this is my granddaughter, Sarah. She and her brother, Chris, live not far from here. And, Sarah, this tall fellow, Tom, is the nephew of the neighbors who live directly behind my house. You know them—my dear friend, Edith, and her husband, Clarence. They had a chance to spend time away from home just after Christmas and into the first two days of January with a relative who lives miles from here. They are going to be able spend part of the time while there attending a huge clan reunion of Clarence's relatives. They asked Edith's nephew, Tom, to come and spend part of his college vacation at their home while they are gone. He would feed their dog and two cats, the caged bird and water their indoor plants. He'd also bring the mail into the house and, in general, make sure all is taken care of at their home while they are away. Edith asked him to also check on me occasionally to make sure I'm all right. He has done that, and even offered to do some grocery shopping for me from a list I could give him. He always comes in the back door since our backyards adjoin each other."

Grandma smiled and then added, "You two get comfortable sitting at the kitchen table while I go get the box with my notes about my contacts with aliens." She hurried into her bedroom and returned with an old-looking covered shoe box. She sat down while placing the box on the table. Then she removed the cover and reached for the first envelope. After that, she placed the lid back on the box and pushed it to the side of the table. Then she extracted the pages from the envelope. She unfolded what she said was the first of eighteen notes. She said that each envelope contained a dated note. Some of the envelopes contained only a paragraph while others contained several pages. With Grandma's nod of approval, Tom began video recording the conversation on his cell phone. Grandma then started reading from her saved note.

Note #1 - 1933, First Encounter

When I was older, I wrote about what I remembered about this day. Here is what I wrote:

Why was Mama so upset? I had just told her of meeting a man in a spaceship hovering over the Earth. Mama was having difficulty accepting such a thing could actually be true. I decided to make it easier for Mama. So, I asked, "Do you suppose it was a dream?"

"Oh, yes," Mama agreed with a huge sigh of relief. "Yes, that's probably what it was. Yes, a dream."

"Well," I answered, "I guess I could have fallen asleep and dreamed it." I said that to soothe Mama, but I felt certain it was not a dream. It had really happened.

"In your dream, what did the spaceman look like?" asked Mama.

"He appeared to be a thin young man. He was wearing a silver-colored jumpsuit. He had brown hair. His eyes were sort of a bright bluish color. He had normal-appearing ears and hands. I noticed his broad thick-looking shoulders. Seems like his neck was short. I really wasn't with him very long. He seemed like a regular human man to me, but there was something different about him that I hadn't noticed in any man I'd seen before. I was puzzled about what it was."

"Interesting," Mama replied. "What did his voice sound like?"

"I don't remember hearing a voice. It was like his mind was sending thoughts to mine which I understood. And I guess my mind was replying in the same way."

"Seems like you had a very interesting dream as you lay out there in the sunshine." Mama smiled. "Do you remember anything else about the man?"

"Oh, I just seemed to know that he was a friend, and I didn't need to be afraid of him." I sighed. *"And yet when he offered to take me for a trip to see other things, I suddenly felt afraid."*

"You sure had an unusual, but fascinating dream, honey. I'm glad you told me about it." Mama gave me a kiss on my forehead.

I hugged Mama and sighed. I felt strongly that the experience I told Mama about was definitely not a dream. It really happened. I had actually met a man from another planet. Yet, it appeared wise to seem to pretend to accept it was only a dream to ease Mama's reaction.

Afterwards when I was alone, I thought again about what I had experienced. My name is Alexia. I was five years old at the time. It was a nice sunny day late in May when the weather was warm enough for Mama to suggest I take a blanket to lay on the ground in the grassy field on the hill just beyond our backyard. Mama thought that the exposure to the sunshine would be healthy for me. There was a steep downgrade from the house to a dry creek bed. On the other side of the creek bed was a steep incline. Mama could look from the back door of the house and see me directly across on the grassy hill, but I wasn't aware of that. I thought I was by myself where nobody could see me on the blanket. I used half the blanket under my body and the other half to cover myself.

As I lay basking in the warm sunshine that day in 1933, I tried to look through the clouds. I had never thought of doing that before. I concentrated very hard. It seemed to me that my spirit lifted out of my body and it rose higher and higher. My spirit passed through the clouds and into the clear blue sky on the other side.

Suddenly, I found myself inside a spaceship. A man was there. I looked around. The walls, ceiling and floor were all a dull white color and constructed of something I wasn't familiar with. I appeared to be in a hall that was curved. It caused my view of my surroundings to be limited. I could not tell how large the spaceship was or if there was any other crew aboard. I did not hear any engine sounds.

The man looked at me very kindly. I could hear his spoken words inside my head rather than with my ears. "You are the first person that I've contacted since I arrived on this planet. All is well here in my spaceship, like the gauges there on the wall indicate." The man pointed beyond my right side. I turned and saw a collection of clear tubes fastened vertically to the wall. I noted they were evenly spaced between each other. There was a total of sixteen tubes in a four-by-four arrangement. The bottom row on the wall was at the level of my shoulders. All of these tubes were half full of some clear liquid. I had never seen gauges like this before without numbers or marks on them. I wondered if the color of the fluid in a tube might change if a problem developed. While I was studying the gauges, the man turned his back towards me. When I again turned towards him, I noticed that he waved his right hand in front of a blank area on the wall, and the area changed from being solid-appearing to being a transparent window. When I looked confused, the man said, "I can control much of my ship with hand motions and mind control."

Then the man said, "Come and look down and see where you came from." I stood before the narrow window, and I gazed with wonder at the Earth below. I could see its blue oceans, brown land masses and white clouds.

"Would you like to take a ride with me?" the friendly man asked. I believed it to be an invitation to view the other planets in our solar system. The thought of being so far from Earth caused me to experience a sudden rush of fear.

"No, I want to go home," I answered. Suddenly, I found myself back on the blanket *on the side of the hill. I felt happy to be back there. I didn't think to wonder until later why I and that man could understand each other. How could that be if he was from a different planet? The two of us probably spoke different languages.*

Once back again on the blanket looking up at the sky, I tried to recall all that had just happened. What impressed me the most about the spaceship man was his friendliness.

Grandma refolded the sheets of paper from which she had just read and placed them back into the envelope.

"That was quite a visit you had, Grandma. Did the idea of life from another planet puzzle you?" asked Sarah.

"No, it just seemed interesting," replied the old woman. "I just accepted what seemed real to me at the time. And later, I had contacts with other non-Earth people."

"Let me go back to the house where I'm staying and get my video camera. It will take a higher quality recording compared to my cell phone. I would like to record your comments about the other-world people," Tom said looking at Grandma as he stood. "I'll be back in just a jiffy."

Grandma smiled as Tom hurriedly left by the back door. She said to Sarah, "When we're finished, I'll ask him to share with me a copy of his cell phone and video recordings."

Grandma sent a loving glance towards Sarah and then added, "I arranged in my will to have these papers given to you if I hadn't shared them with you in person earlier. I'm so glad we can talk about this now. I've thought several times of giving them to you while you were here on one of your visits with me, but then I'd get sidetracked. I was glad knowing no matter what happens, you'd get this box sooner or later."

CHAPTER TWO

Once Tom set up the video camera, Grandma talked more about her childhood life. Days came and went. She hadn't thought of her spaceman friend for some time. Kindergarten and the new friends she met there took up much of her attention. Life seemed full. She felt safe and happy. And then, one Saturday that changed.

Grandma took another envelope from the shoe box. She started reading aloud the words on the pages.

Note #2 – Spring 1934, The Butterfly

I was six years old. I was alone in my backyard. It was a bright sunny day. I noticed a huge magnificent butterfly. It was larger and more beautiful than any butterfly I'd ever seen before. The colors were outstanding. It was just a short distance north of our yard. I knew it was against our family rules for me go past the yard, but a thought came to me indicating it surely wouldn't hurt to take a couple of steps beyond the edge of the yard to get closer to view the butterfly.

I stood very close to the butterfly which was perched on top of a green plant. I admired its lovely blue color with various red, yellow and violet designs on its wings. Suddenly, the top of the left wing of the butterfly started to fade.

Whoa! I was alarmed.

"Oh, all right," I heard inside my head. I suddenly sensed that there was man standing behind me. I somehow knew that he was a spaceman in a spiritual body, not in a physical one. I was relieved and sighed happily when the butterfly wing became whole again. I blinked.

Then I found myself leaving our yard and walking on the nearby path beside the road heading north. My feet were moving without any thought from me. In fact, I had no choice. My body was moving automatically, and there seemed no way to stop it. This was something very odd. Then, I saw two neighbor women whom I knew talking to each other. "Turn around and go back home," one of the women said to me. "You know you aren't supposed to be this far away from your yard." Yes, I acknowledged with a nod, but kept going. Indeed, I had no choice. I couldn't stop what my body was doing.

I kept walking north. Then, I saw a lady wearing a white dress standing next to the path. "You should go back home," this woman said kindly, but there was no power in her words. I just kept going. The path ahead of me split into a Y. I took the branch on the right, but for some reason, changed my mind and walked back a few paces and took the path going to the left.

Ahead, I saw a big silver-colored disk-shaped spaceship beside a tall oak tree. I noticed that it hovered just above the ground without any visible support.

As I walked closer, I noticed three of what might be high school-age boys. They all seemed to be about the same height. There was an energy or something about them that seemed more boyish than adult-like. I noticed each of them was wearing the same pattern of clothes. About chest high, the fabric changed to be of a lighter weight and shinier appearance than the lower part of the garments. The top of the outfits seemed rather dressy. I continued walking past them.

In my mind, I heard the words, "She's getting away."

A deeper voice replied, "No, I have full control."

I wasn't aware of anything else until I found myself back on a path. This was not the same place where I started my walk. I did not know exactly where I was or in which direction was home. My feet started moving *without me even thinking about it. The slope of the path leveled out when I came to a section of houses. I noticed a sidewalk next to a paved street. I started walking on the sidewalk. I kept walking until realizing I had walked around the block. I thought there must be an exit. I'd better walk around the block again and be more observant this time.*

As I repeated my walk around the block, I noticed a side street on the opposite side of the road from where I was. I took the side street which then brought me to a busy main street. Where was I? I peered more closely at my surroundings. "Oh," I whispered aloud, "I know this street. I can get home from here."

I hadn't gone far when I noticed my Uncle Fred coming toward me. I felt so happy to see him. He was delighted and seemed relieved when he noticed me. He told me that I had been gone from home for three hours or more, and my parents were super worried. They had phoned him to come and help find me. They couldn't imagine what had happened to me.

I was very warmly welcomed when I arrived home. I had fully expected to be punished for disobeying the rule not to leave the yard when playing outside. Instead, I was receiving hugs and being told of the relief to find me safe. Mama was concerned about a new small swollen place below the center of my forehead. I didn't know it was there. Mama wondered if perhaps I had fallen or something. I said I didn't know why the mark was there. Then I wondered silently why I'd used the word MARK instead of BRUISE.

When my parents asked me where I had been for the past three hours, I told them that I thought I hurt my head, and I could not remember where I had been. I told them that I remembered the butterfly and walking on a path, and the next thing I could remember was seeing Uncle Fred. Because of Mama's prior reaction, I did not mention the spaceman.

Sometime later when I was alone, I found myself thinking of the experience with the butterfly and the spaceman. This spaceman was not the same one who showed me the view of the Earth from his spaceship. This second spaceman had somehow compelled me to leave my yard. I wondered how he projected his personality to where I was. That's what I finally decided he'd done when I thought about it.

Alexia pulled another envelope from the box. This one was a light brown envelope. She opened the envelope and pulled out a folded paper. She unfolded the paper and started to read what it said:

Note #3 – Spring 1934, My Cat's Response

My gray cat noticed a difference about me. She seemed disturbed about the new spot on my forehead. While I was sitting on the sofa watching a television program, the cat climbed onto my shoulder and stretched her neck to smell the spot. Then she tried to paw it off. Naturally, I stopped this behavior. For the next two days, my cat periodically tried to reach my forehead spot and then scratch if off. I stopped this behavior. Finally, my cat accepted the spot and then ignored it.

Grandma stopped reading. She smiled and then said, "There is more to my story, but how about us each having a bowl of vanilla ice cream and a glazed donut while I continue telling you of my memories." Tom turned the switch to OFF on the recording machine.

CHAPTER THREE

Grandma savored some of the ice cream and took two bites of a glazed donut. Then she motioned to Tom to again turn the video camera on. She double checked and noted the recording light showed the camera was operating. Grandma smiled and began reading more about her past from the contents of still another envelope.

Note #4 – 1940, The Evil Face

A few years after my experience which I thought of as The Butterfly Day, my family was living in a different location. This time it was in a flat valley. We lived in a house beside a city street not far from the edge of town. My sister, Marsha, was now five years old and in kindergarten. My brother, seven-year-old Lawrence, was in second grade. I was then twelve years old and in the seventh grade.

On a bright moonlit evening, all of my family had gone to bed at our regular time. I had my own small room, while Marsha and Lawrence shared a larger room. I was awakened in the middle of the night by the sense of something evil in my room. I opened my eyes. Floating in the air just below the ceiling, a gray face stared down at me. The face seemed evil and threatening. Then the face grew larger and seemed to fill the upper half of the room. I suddenly felt I had to get away from it. I fled out the front door of the house.

I was surprised to find Marsha and Lawrence on the front porch steps. They told me they had also been frightened by a big, scary face, and they ran out of the house. Both of them were fully dressed in everyday clothes. I noticed that I was as well and didn't remember changing out of my nightgown. Lawrence had a flashlight in his hand.

Marsha's shoelace was untied. I leaned over to tie it, then stood. We felt compelled to walk to the edge of town and enter a large nearby field. We saw a large spaceship ahead. It hovered about two feet above the ground with no visible support. Two steps led to a door. We felt compelled to climb the steps to board the spaceship.

Then, it seemed suddenly we were back home. Marsha said we needed to tell Mama what had happened. I said for Marsha and Lawrence to go to bed and I would do the telling. I went into the bedroom of my parents. I whispered, "Mama?" She woke up and looked at me.

I started to tell Mama of our trip to the spaceship, but what came out of my mouth was telling of the fear of the horrible face floating in the air in my bedroom. I told how it had frightened me so much. Daddy was awake by then. He looked concerned and asked questions about what he assumed was a bad dream.

Nothing was said about it the next morning. As I thought about it later, I became puzzled. What had stopped me from being able to tell my parents about all the events of what had happened last night? I noted that Marsha and Lawrence each had a new forehead mark, but they had no memory of an evil-appearing face in their room, of having a mark placed on their forehead, or of seeing a spaceship. I wondered why I could remember the evil face and the spaceship, but my brother and sister couldn't.

Grandma stopped talking and noted the facial expressions of her listeners. They were fascinated by what she had read. Grandma very much enjoyed telling these interested listeners more of her story. She picked up another envelope.

Note #5 – 1948 to 1949, Family Losses

The years slipped by. Marsha died due to complications of pneumonia when she was 13 years old. Lawrence died as a passenger in a horrible auto accident the following year. My parents had deeply grieved the loss of their two children. Then, being the only surviving child of our family, the bond between my parents and me grew even stronger. I missed my sister and brother so much.

Note #6 – 1950 to 1952, First Pregnancy Loss

I fell in love and married a wonderful man, my soul mate. A few months later, my doctor confirmed that I was pregnant. My husband, Mark, and I were delighted. When I was about three months pregnant, I had the urge to go for a walk in a different direction than I'd gone before. I came across a woman with a preschool-age boy. The mother said her *son was recovering from the measles. I wondered if the boy was still in the contagious stage. But, I decided, the mother wouldn't allow him to be where he might infect others if she thought he was still contagious. When I developed symptoms of the measles about ten days later, I was surprised. I was also a little angry at the mother whose carelessness of allowing her son to be where he could infect others had caused me to come down with the measles. I had somehow avoided getting them earlier.*

I felt sick and decided to stay in bed while Mark went to work one morning. I fell asleep. When I awoke, I suddenly knew that I was no longer pregnant, yet there was no evidence of an actual miscarriage. At the time, I thought that the measles had caused the loss of the pregnancy. This pregnancy loss devastated Mark and me. It was only later that I came to believe that my fetus was taken by the space people.

Note #7 – 1953, Second Pregnancy Loss

Some months passed before Mark and I decided to try for another baby. I became pregnant again. The pregnancy was normal until Mark and I were moving into a larger home. I was eleven weeks pregnant when I went down the flight of stairs at the old house many times while carrying heavy boxes. When only a few more things were left to be taken out of the place, I was alarmed while walking up the front porch steps to feel a sudden sharp pain in my abdomen. I had only one last trip to make before all the things to be moved would be out of the residence. Mark was busy loading the items into a rented trailer. I went into the house. Suddenly, I felt cramps in my abdomen and lower back. I felt like I needed to have a bowel movement. I went directly to the bathroom and sat on the toilet. The cramps increased in severity and frequency. Suddenly, I realized I was having a miscarriage. I knew that this was a real miscarriage, not a pregnancy loss caused by the aliens taking the fetus from me. But once again, Mark and I grieved the loss of an unborn child.

Five months after the miscarriage, Mark and I decided to try again to have a baby. This time we were successful. Mark and I felt happy. (MUCH Later Additional Note: As time passed, we had four children. Eventually we became grandparents when Chris was born in 1999, and Sarah was born in 2001.)

Alexia stopped talking and used a spoon as she scooped the remaining now soft ice cream from her bowl. Sarah stood, went to the kitchen, and then brought three glasses of water and the bag of the remaining glazed donuts to the table.

CHAPTER FOUR

Encouraged to tell more, Grandma Alexia smiled and then mentioned that when she was about 30 years old, sightings of spacecraft were more frequently reported in the news. People called them "flying saucers," because they resembled the shape of a saucer. Another common term was UFO, meaning "Unidentified Flying Object."

Grandma selected the next envelope and continued reading.

Note #8 – 1960, Hypnotism Offer #1

When I was about 32 years old, I read a library book about brief abductions of humans by the crews of the flying saucers. This same author published later books about what people told him of their experiences with these aliens. I sent a letter to the author in care of his publisher's address. I soon received a reply. I sent a letter back telling a little of my experience with the aliens. The author was intrigued. He offered to find a hypnotist in my area and pay the fee for the procedure. He would be present during my hypnotism. He would ask questions and record my responses about my experiences including my time inside the spaceship. I refused the offer. For some reason, I felt terrified of being hypnotized. This wasn't logical, but the feeling was intense.

Note #9 – 1962, Forehead Marks

I remembered reading a magazine article about visitors from outer space. The article claimed that the aliens were kidnapping Earth men, women, and children for a few hours. The purpose of these abductions was unknown to the victims. These victims had a sense of missing time, but they had no memory of what happened during that time. Afterwards, they discovered that they had a new tiny bump on their foreheads a short distance above their noses. The small affected area seemed to blend into the coloring of the forehead's skin and did not call attention to itself.

After reading that, I gazed at my own forehead tiny bump in the mirror. I began to observe other people and to look for the telltale forehead mark. I noticed that just a very few men, women, and children had one.

Note #10 – 1965, Hypnotism Offer #2

When I was about 37 years old, I read a second book on the subject of alien abductions. Because of the similarities to my own experiences, I wanted to learn more. As I had done after reading the first book some years ago, I sent a letter to the author of this book. I mentioned that I noticed I had the same type of forehead mark above my nose *that the author in his book described were found on alien abductees. I previously hadn't thought much or worried about the very slightly swollen place located on my own forehead.*

Like the author of the first book, the author of the second book wrote back and offered to make an appointment in my area with a hypnotist for me. He would pay the fee. The result would be that I would remember more fully the details of my experience and perhaps remember how the forehead mark was created. The book author would be present and be able to ask me questions while I was under the hypnotic spell. For some reason, AGAIN the idea of being hypnotized frightened me. I wrote back to the book author and politely refused his offer. I was completely puzzled why TWICE I seemed prevented from revealing details of my experiences regarding contact with the UFO people.

Grandma Alexia paused while telling of her past. Then she expressed regret that she hadn't accepted at least one of the offers made by these two authors. She wouldn't have minded later if her experiences were included in the respective author's later future books regarding alien abductions.

Tom said, "Gee, you missed a good opportunity to learn more about what happened. I wonder why you felt frightened about being hypnotized. Perhaps the idea was implanted in your mind not to reveal all you'd learned about those from the other planet."

Alexia blinked and then slowly nodded her head. She picked up another envelope and read what it said to Sarah and Tom.

Note #11 – 1970, A Daughter's Funeral

I particularly recall one time of sensing a psychic communication from my alien contact. I was about 42 years old at the time.

I was given to know that my daughter, whom I had lost when I was three months pregnant, was actually taken by the aliens as a fetus. My daughter was born healthy and grew up on the alien planet, but had recently died at the age of eighteen years old. Once I understood this, I found myself transported psychically to the alien planet in order to attend my daughter's funeral. It was the alien custom to reduce a dead body to ashes before being launched by a cannon into the sky. The body's ashes would then resettle onto the planet's surface and fertilize the soil. Friends of the deceased stood nearby and sadly watched the proceedings. I grieved the loss of this child a second time. I had previously grieved the ending of my first pregnancy years ago. After the ceremony, my psychic self was returned home.

It seemed to me that the people on the other planet were different than humans on Earth. The women at the funeral for my daughter seemed to be dressed alike. I wondered if this clothing was a uniform or if it was the standard dress code for women living on that planet. They appeared to share a thread of common awareness. It seemed they were each like a single cell in a giant organism. I sensed all of these women weren't independent separate individuals, but were connected somehow to a large group *telepathically. If I had become a resident of that planet, would I have lost some of my sense of individuality?*

Note #12 – 1979, A Declining Population

One of the aliens communicated to me that they were concerned about their severely declining population. I learned that the aliens were using human *females to help expand their population. I was told that a human egg cell was impregnated with sperm from an alien using technology unknown to Earth humans. After a specified time, the developing fetus would be removed painlessly from the mother's womb and then transported to the planet far away. The mother would know nothing of this process except the realization that she was no longer pregnant. The fetus would continue to develop in an alien artificial womb. This process occurred only once to an individual woman, but it occurred to many different women over a prolonged period of time. All this was done without the awareness of Earth people.*

CHAPTER FIVE

Grandma Alexia took a bite of her donut. Then she continued reading to her two fascinated listeners. She said that calendar pages were flipped and years went by.

Note #13 – 1983, Disappearing Treasures

I called my friend from outer space, the first alien that I met when I was five years old, by the name of Spaceman. Sometimes I felt his spiritual presence briefly near me. It seemed to me that he had tasks to do which kept him occupied, and so he was not able to visit me frequently.

One day, I was pleased to sense the very strong presence of Spaceman. I was then 55 years old. I had felt his presence numerous times in the past, but this time, my awareness of him was stronger than usual. He said that he needed to leave Earth to go back to his home planet. He communicated to me that other alien beings would contact me from time to time. He was telling me goodbye and that he had enjoyed our longtime friendship. I was greatly impressed that he cared enough about me to let me know he was going back to his home. He had been on Earth for about 50 years.

Additional incidents occurred during this same time period. Mark and I had moved to a different home. Our new residence had a spare bedroom where some items were stored until we could get everything organized. A red-top table with chrome legs was located in the spare bedroom near the door. I placed some of my important items on the table where I would be sure to find them. Later, I'd find a permanent place for these things. Among these items was my address book which I placed near the edge of the table top.

A few days later, I was extremely frustrated when I needed the address book and it wasn't where I left it! I was positive I'd put it on the table. Mark said he hadn't touched it. Then, about ten days after the address book had disappeared, it was back. It wasn't in the same exact spot, but quite near where I had left it. This was puzzling. Where had it gone and how had it come back? I was sure I hadn't imagined it was missing. By then, I had a secure spot to store the address book in another part of the house.

I started unpacking a box that had been left in the spare room. I removed a framed family photo from this box. I planned to put the photo on top of the dresser in the master bedroom, but was interrupted by a phone call. I laid the picture on the corner of the red table when I went to answer the phone. I was sidetracked for the rest of the day. I felt confused and upset the next day when I discovered the framed photograph that I had placed on the table was gone. Why was this happening? About ten days later, the missing item was back on the table top.

I desperately spoke aloud, "What is going on?"

In an ESP reply, a young woman answered. "We are duplicating some of your special things so you'll have them when you move here with us. While we had your items for a few days, we made a copy of them, and then returned the originals to you. Only a limited number of Earth humans will be invited to travel with us to our home planet during the current times. Other chosen humans will be invited to join us later when the time is appropriate."

WHAT? I was startled.

No more ESP conversation followed.

Later, I placed a book on the corner of the table. It was a fictional story about aliens visiting Earth. The book disappeared from that particular corner of the table. About five days later, I sent an ESP message to the *young woman who had contacted me earlier. I said, "I don't care much about that book. You can keep it." The book never reappeared on the table top. Nothing else was placed on that corner of the table.*

Note #14 – 1986, Thoughts & Observations

When I was about 58 years old, I had a dream. In my dream, there were many spaceships in the sky. They were hovering over Earth getting ready to pick up the people with the forehead mark. A mechanism on the spaceships would identify and then transport up the chosen people. Once a spaceship had a full passenger load, it would fly away and another spaceship would take its place. In the dream, something terrible was about to happen to Earth, and people were being evacuated before it occurred. Those to be airlifted to safety were to be transported to the home planet of the spaceship crews.

There was very seldom any conversation in my environment about UFOs or about people from another planet visiting Earth. Over the past twenty-five years or so, there was high interest in NASA space missions. In the 1960s and 1970s, public interest was captivated by the Apollo moon missions. In the late 1980s to the early 2000s, public interest was focused on the flights of the Space Shuttle astronauts. I was impressed to see that the photos of Earth taken by the NASA astronauts from space were exactly the same as my memory of the view of Earth from the alien spacecraft when I was five years old.

Is there life on other planets? Remembering back to when I first met Spaceman, Earth people I knew at that time didn't even consider whether there is life on other planets. But I have no doubt that there is life on at least one other planet. I feel certain there are human-like people somewhere in the universe who are more scientifically advanced than Earth humans.

The alien beings that I encountered appeared human. They did not have the huge head pictured in some cartoons which show outer space people. But, I thought, a cartoon artist was having fun drawing something to attract the interest of viewers, and it didn't have to be a true picture.

I never had the opportunity to take a photograph of Spaceman, so I made a drawing of him. It showed a face with a smile. He had a nose that looked like it could have been part of an Earthly face. The placement of the two eyes on the face was somehow different, but not much, than what Earthly humans have. Spaceman had eyes with pupils of a bright color of blue. He seemed to have a slight brownish cast to his complexion. He was shorter than many of the men of Earth, but not as short as some. He had a body build that wasn't slight, but wasn't huge either. One of the differences I noted between the people I saw from the other planet and those of Earth was the strong yet invisible energy field, or aura, that surrounded the bodies of the aliens. Even though it was invisible, I could still sense its presence. It seemed to me that these people communicated with each other via mental telepathy. I never heard them make vocal sounds. Interestingly, when I was contacted via telepathy by the aliens, I comprehended it perfectly and even responded in the same way.

I was surprised when unknown-to-me aliens attempted to contact me. The first contacts were from men, but later a woman silently conversed with me from time to time. The woman didn't say what her name was, but I began thinking of the lady as Angela. She seemed to be a woman of about twenty-eight years old.

I wondered if I had been brainwashed into feeling an intense friendliness towards the first spaceman I'd met. As I thought about it, I felt convinced there was a friendly tie between Spaceman and me. Otherwise, he wouldn't have made the effort to check on me *in a psychic way from time to time and to make the special effort to tell me goodbye. In spite of my not knowing the reasons for the temporary abductions, I believed that all of the aliens visiting Earth had friendly intentions towards humans. Why would I believe that these aliens, who were abducting people for their own purposes, be considered friendly? That didn't seem logical, but I still sensed the friendliness.*

CHAPTER SIX

Alexia stopped talking and took a sip of water from her glass. Tom and Sarah were sorry and felt quite surprised when Grandma Alexia said it was her bedtime and she felt tired. She added that maybe Tom and Sarah could use Sarah's car to go up the side street to the parking area at the top of the hill. From there, they'd be able to watch the fireworks that would be shot up into the sky when midnight came and the New Year arrived.

Rather than watching the fireworks, Sarah said she'd rather go where Tom was staying, and continue to read Grandma's saved notes. Sarah was worried that, if they stayed at Grandma's house, their talking would keep the old woman awake. Tom said he was glad he and Sarah were going to spend more time together in the nearby warm house. He didn't want to go up the hill in the cold to watch the fireworks.

Sarah said she would slip in through Grandma's back door later that night. After saying she'd have to leave early in the morning to be available for the babysitting for her friends that she promised to do, Sarah hugged her very dear grandmother and then said, "I know you normally sleep until shortly before 9 AM. I'll be gone by eight o'clock. There is no need for you to set your clock's alarm in order to get up in time to see me leave. Instead, I will tell you goodnight and also goodbye now. Do have a really good sleep, Grandma, and have an especially Happy New Year."

Alexia felt very tired and went to bed after Sarah and Tom left. It was New Year's Eve—the last day of 2021. She didn't feel the urge to stay up to see the New Year of 2022 start. She was happy she'd given the box of her saved *The Earth Visitor* written memories to Sarah. She was delighted that Sarah seemed to be so happy to receive them.

Alexia, then in bed, rolled onto her right side, closed her eyes, and thought of Spaceman. Then, she smiled as she thought of her dear husband, Mark, who had died four years ago. Sometime during the night, Alexia died peacefully in her sleep. She was 93 years old.

Sarah had left the back door unlocked before she went with Tom so that she could come back in without waking Grandma. She forgot to relock it when she came in later that night. She exited Grandma's home via the front door when she left early the next morning.

Tom called Sarah mid-afternoon with very sad news. He said that he had gone to Grandma's house to deliver some groceries.

There was no response when he pushed the buzzer at the back door. He entered the home when he found the back door unlocked. He called out to Grandma, but received no answer. He searched for her room by room until he discovered Grandma in bed where she was laying peacefully in death.

Tom found Grandma's list of phone numbers on the open shelf of her nightstand. He called emergency services and then called Sarah.

Sarah was devastated by the loss of her beloved grandmother. At Alexia's funeral, family members and friends took turns telling stories of their memories about her. Alexia had lived a long and productive life, and she would be missed by all her knew her.

CHAPTER SEVEN

Saddened Sarah was determined to honor her grandmother's memory by carefully organizing all the data Grandma had given her about the visiting aliens. Sarah was enchanted by what she had read so far of what her grandmother had shared.

Several days after the funeral, Sarah opened the old-looking covered shoe box her grandmother had given her. It contained many envelopes. Taped to the inside of the lid was a short pink envelope addressed with the words FOR SARAH. With tingling fingers, she opened the unsealed envelope and pulled out a handwritten note. She read:

My Dear Sarah,

I have saved my many notes about Spaceman and related subjects to give to you when you are an adult because of your intelligent questions as a child. You once asked me why couldn't there be life on other planets. I didn't feel free then to tell you of my own experiences regarding that subject, but I've made arrangements to share my notes about them with you when you are older. Because you were so talkative as a child, I was afraid about what you would have told others had I shared with you this information before you were older. I'm pleased to now share this with the adult person you have become. Note that those from outer space who visited Earth were careful not to interfere with the conditions here or how people born on Earth live their lives. I hope you are able to make good use of what you will now be reading. Perhaps you will feel inclined to use these notes to write a book to share the information with others. I'd like it if you did that.

The note ended with the words, *With much love to my very dear grandchild.* Grandma had signed it in the normal way she always did when writing notes to her grandchildren, but this time beneath that, she added her signature using her official legal name. Sarah had tears in her eyes when she finished reading the note.

After the tears dried, Sarah pulled out another envelope and continued to read.

Note #15 – 1987, Spaceman's Planet

Spaceman never did tell me the name or location of his home planet. He did tell me that his planet was the largest of three planets orbiting its sun. The three planets were about the same distance apart from each other as the Earth is from its neighboring planet of Mars. Spaceman told me the people on the large planet where he lived liked to engage in commercial trade with the people on the two smaller planets.

I found a book at the local city library about astronomy. This book included several pages of photographs of planets outside our own solar system which were taken by the Hubble Space Telescope. I noted one large planet with two nearby smaller ones, and I wondered if my spaceman friend had come from that area.

I thought more about Spaceman and wondered how he had adapted to Earth over these many years. What had Spaceman been eating? How did he get his food? Was he giving himself injections of some type each day? Did he have some way to create water to drink?

Note #16 – 1988, A New Friend

When I was about 60 years old, I felt the presence of someone. "Who are you?" I asked while thinking it was weird knowing someone was there that I couldn't see with my human eyes. My black cat, who had been standing next to me, hissed. He looked towards the window of the room. I saw that and looked there too.

I noticed what seemed to be a subtle light in the shape of a man. I rubbed my eyes and looked again. Then I felt rather than heard a greeting. He said that he was friend. The man told me that he was assigned to keep tabs on me until it was my turn to be transported to the other planet which was to be my permanent home. He added that I would feel his presence from time to time, but not to feel frightened. After communicating his message, the man disappeared.

Sarah wondered if Spaceman was still alive on his own planet. Could she somehow reach him by mental telepathy? How would she go about it? She decided it would be best to check the Internet to see if there was a procedure to contact another person by mental telepathy. It took time finding and then studying the instructions on this Internet site. She tried several times to reach Spaceman in this way, but had no luck. "Well, he is probably dead by now," Sarah said aloud to herself. "Or maybe I'm not making contact in the correct way."

Sarah decided she was going to need a special place to record her own thoughts as well as keeping a record regarding the verbal stories that Grandma had shared about the aliens. What would be the best way to do that? Sarah remembered seeing a hardcovered book with totally blank pages inside for sale at a local store. Yes, she'd go there and buy one of those. On the first page, she'd print a title for the book. She decided to call it *The Earth Visitor,* which is the name Grandma Alexia had said she would use if she ever wrote a book about her alien friend. Sarah also decided to scan Grandma's notes and create a file on her computer. She would place the original paper pages in clear plastic protectors and place them chronologically in a binder. Sarah noticed how the handwriting of Grandma's notes changed over time. The later notes were written more firmly than the earlier ones, and they added more details.

Sarah's thoughts were interrupted when someone knocked on the front door. It turned out to be her friend, Amy.

As the two friends sat at the kitchen table with cups of hot tea before them, Sarah asked Amy if she knew anyone who ever saw a man from outer space.

Amy asked curiously, "Why do you ask?"

Sarah told her dear friend about the many envelopes with the interesting notes that her grandmother, Alexia, had written during previous years.

"Do you believe there are people living on a faraway planet?" Amy asked.

"Well, my grandmother certainly did, and I always have been able trust her judgement. Yes, I do think there could be life on more than one planet." Sarah sighed. "I have more pages to read of what Grandma wrote."

The two friends went into the living room and sat facing each other on the sofa. The conversation barely got started when Sarah's cell phone rang. The call was from Sarah's brother, Chris. He said his car's gas tank was empty. He was in a store parking lot about a 15-minute drive from Sarah. Could she come in her car and bring him the filled gasoline can he had saved in the garage for the lawn mower? He gave her directions how to find his stalled car. Of course, Sarah agreed to help him.

When Amy heard what the phone call was about, she said, "I'm truly looking forward to hearing about what happened to your grandmother. I'll look forward to our future conversation, but I'll leave now so you can help your brother."

CHAPTER EIGHT

When Sarah had available time away from her busy work and social schedule, she was finally able to resume reading Grandma's notes. Sarah picked up a white envelope. Very carefully, Sarah reached into this envelope and pulled out the papers enclosed.

Note #17- 1998, Misplaced Affection

It was a sunny day when I went to the store. I was nearly 70 years old. I was suddenly reminded of Spaceman when I saw an elderly man with a similar complexion and gait walking towards me. He was headed in the opposite direction than I was going. My whole being seemed to suddenly transfer the deep affection I felt for Spaceman to the man coming towards me. When he and I were only a few steps apart, I suddenly reached out both of my arms and hugged him tightly. This was an automatic reaction. I wouldn't have done it if I had time to think about it.

"Oh, I'm so glad to see you," I said to the man.

"What? Who are you?" asked the shocked man.

"Oh, I'm so sorry. You remind me of someone I consider special. Sorry, sorry." I answered.

"Well, whoever he is, I envy him," the stranger said to me. He added, "Can we sit someplace, and you can tell me about this special person?"

As it turned out, this new man in my life found ways to seemingly accidentally be shopping in the same store at the same time that I was. I generally went there a half hour or so before noon on Thursdays. When we saw each other again, I accepted his invitation to join him for a coffee break in the store's small corner cafeteria. Subsequent visits became longer conversations over lunch. He said his name was Carl. He lived alone since the recent death of his ailing wife. For me, it was nice to see this man who reminded me of Spaceman.

Once Carl learned that I was married, he very tactfully started to ask probing questions regarding my current financial situation. Finally, he said, "My dear, we have grown to have a close relationship. I'd like to marry you after you file and receive a divorce. You should be careful in having your part of the joint marriage properties divided fairly. If you can, during the property settlement, get the rental house that you and your husband own transferred into only your legal name. You and I could move there after we get married."

I looked into Carl's face. Yes, he was totally serious. I had no idea our friendship had reached this point. How could he possibly know of the rental Mark and I owned? Likely, I had mentioned it during one of the conversations I'd had with Carl.

Still feeling shocked about his marriage proposal, I responded, "Oh, Carl, I'm so sorry. I thought we were just friends. I love my husband deeply. I don't want a divorce. I'm afraid we have come to a point when it would be kinder to say goodbye." I stood up, ready to walk away from Carl.

"Please don't go," pleaded Carl. "I don't want to say goodbye." He paused and then added, "I promise I won't mention marriage again." He said that in a sincere tone of voice, but I began to question his real intentions. Carl left the table and stood in front of me. He reached his arms towards me, then he pulled me in a strong hug towards his chest.

I paused. I stood passive for a moment while trying to decide what the kindest thing I could do for Carl in these circumstances would be. I decided a strong firm goodbye would be best.

Carl appeared upset when I suddenly pulled away from him, turned and walked rapidly away. I stopped shopping in the same store where Carl was accustomed to seeing me. I never saw him again. Nor did I ever see anyone again who reminded me of Spaceman.

Sarah sighed. Why, she wondered, had her grandmother felt such a strong feeling of affection when she first saw Carl? Why didn't her grandmother more quickly recognize him as the scheming man he was? Well yes, he did suddenly remind her of her longtime trusted absent Spaceman friend, and that did probably trigger memories and sudden feelings of affection and trust.

Sarah pulled out another envelope and continued to read.

Note #18 – Fall 2021, The Final Chapter

I know that, in my advanced years, I do not have much time left. This does not make me sad. I know that my health is declining, and I often feel very tired. I am grateful for the many blessings I've had in my life. I have been surrounded by those I love. I've been able to accomplish my important goals. Death of my body seems to me to be a time of rest, but not the end of the inner soul.

I think about the outer space people from time to time. I feel fortunate to have had contact with them throughout my life, and it has been my privilege to know them. I remember the last sudden burst upon my consciousness of the man who had been the one who seemed assigned to communicate with me regarding the other planet. This last contact was less than three months ago. He was very cheerful when he asked if I was ready to leave Earth and be transported to the other planet. I gave him a strong negative reply. I feel that it is now just too late to go. I am now an old frail woman. The man seemed disappointed. Then, suddenly he was gone, but there seemed an echo of sadness in the air.

Two days after I refused to leave Earth, I heard on my kitchen radio that six spacecraft had been detected far out over the Pacific Ocean. They were hovering there for only a short time, and then instantly disappeared. The description given about them seemed indicate they were more advanced than anything known produced on Earth. The newscaster asked, "Could they be spacecraft from another planet?" Then he laughed and went on to another topic. I suddenly knew that I could have been on one of those spacecrafts. Had I made a mistake in deciding not to leave Earth?

I wonder what my life would have been like if I had been transported to the other planet during my young adult life. Still, if I had been, I wouldn't have met my dear husband nor had the children I was blessed to have. I've had a happy life here on Earth, and I might not have liked living on the other planet.

CHAPTER NINE

Sarah's cell phone rang. The call was from Amy who said her grandmother was visiting and had a mark on her forehead. Amy wondered if Sarah would like to drive the few miles to come see it.

Amy opened her door when Sarah stepped up onto Amy's wide front porch. Obviously, Amy was looking forward to visiting with her friend.

"Oh, I'm so glad you were able to come on such short notice. Let me introduce you to my grandmother and also to my cousin, Jack, who brought her here." Amy smiled to herself. The real reason she wanted her dear friend to come was to meet Jack. Amy knew that her grandmother's forehead mark didn't look similar to Sarah's grandma's forehead mark as it had been described.

Sarah followed Amy into the living room and was introduced to the woman covered by a blanket while sitting on the sofa.

"You can call me Grandmother Rose, if you wish," the woman with white hair said. "It would be easier than trying to pronounce my long foreign sounding last name."

"Where is Jack?" Amy asked.

"Oh, he is out walking your dog. He'll be back shortly," answered her grandmother. "You said your friend would be interested in the mark on my forehead. Let her look at it now."

Sarah came close to the frail-appearing old woman. The forehead's swollen spot was actually rather ugly in Sarah's opinion. It protruded outwardly about an eighth of an inch. It had a slight grayish color. It was about half an inch square.

"No," Sarah said. "It doesn't match the forehead mark my grandma had." Gazing more closely, Sarah frowned. "This one is a larger size and has a tint to it which wasn't present in my grandma's mark."

"I became very self-conscious about the swollen place in full view whenever anyone looked at me when I was a teenager," Grandmother Rose remarked. "It started as a sore when I fell off my bicycle. It didn't seem to reduce in size as time went by. My parents finally took me to a plastic surgeon and asked that it be removed. I was about fifteen years old then. The surgeon was skeptical about doing that for some reason. SO---I didn't get rid of the awful awareness of it."

Sarah smiled and commented, "At least you had something that no one else did. It made you stand out more as an individual. That helped others remember you more easily."

"Hump," replied the old woman. "I'd rather not be remembered that way." And then she smiled and added, "But it did make a reason for me to meet you. I can see why Amy likes you so much."

Conversation flowed easily after that. Sarah was glad she'd come. When Jack entered the room, he and Sarah were introduced. Amy saw only a friendly exchange of glances between Sarah and Jack.

Amy spoke up saying, "Well, sit on the other end of the sofa from Grandmother, Jack, and then join us in our conversation. Sarah was telling us of a mark on the forehead of her grandmother that seemed to have been put there by someone from outer space."

"That's interesting," Jack replied. "I have a friend who claims the mark on his father's forehead was a mystery until he heard that similar marks were seen on other foreheads. His father then accepted it as a normal thing."

"Go sit down and then let's talk about this," requested Amy.

Once seated, Jack asked, "Why is the mark on some foreheads a subject you said you'd been talking about before I arrived?"

Grandmother Rose replied, "Sarah was given her Grandmother Alexia's notes about various contacts with those from another planet. The forehead marks are mentioned in the notes Sarah now has."

"Interesting," replied Jack. "My friend claims his father didn't remember why his mark appeared. He thought it would disappear in time, but it never did. The mark was small and didn't bother him, so he just left it alone. Later, he saw a similar mark on a couple of other foreheads. One was on a woman and the other on a man."

"Did anyone you know mention when and why the marks appeared?" asked Amy.

"Not that I heard of," replied Jack. "Nor did I stop to wonder about it. I realize now that I should have asked more questions. I just took it for granted like it was a normal thing of nature. Maybe it was caused by an insect bite or something."

Sarah replied, "My grandma indicated the marks were placed on the foreheads of humans by the people from outer space. She also mentioned that these marks were located on the forehead a little distance above the nose of a person. Does this coincide with what you heard, Jack?"

"I didn't learn much about the whole subject, but none of what you just said was ever denied by what I heard," replied Jack. "I wonder if there are any books at public libraries discussing visitors coming from another planet and what they might have done while on Earth."

CHAPTER TEN

"Well, enough of this chatter," sighed Grandmother Rose looking at Jack. "Tell us what your brother, Sam, is up to."

"Talking about flying saucers," started Jack, "Sam had a traumatic experience as a child. He saw a flying saucer and told his classmates about it. But his classmates didn't believe him and bullied him mercilessly. As a result, Sam became depressed, pulled away from people, and gravitated to animals, especially horses.

"So now, Sam can talk for hours about horses, but will not talk about flying saucers. Let me tell you about the horse Sam recently acquired.

"Sam was driving on the highway when there was a multi-vehicle crash just ahead of him. Luckily, Sam was not directly involved

The Earth Visitor and Alexia

in the accident himself, but was caught in the resulting stalled traffic. He got out of his car and walked ahead to see if anyone might need help. He saw a damaged horse trailer behind a pickup truck. Inside the trailer was a bay-colored horse with a black mane and tail. Sam was standing near the trailer and heard what the horse owner said to his companion. The owner said the horse had suffered a broken leg. He felt it would be humane to have the horse euthanized to prevent its suffering. Sam shook his head and then spoke up."

Jack continued. "Sam said he asked the horse owner not to shoot the animal, but instead to give it to Sam who promised he would work with the broken leg and take good care of horse. He explained that he lived on a farm where the horse could easily be pastured. Sam added that he really liked horses and that he would take good care of this one."

Jack added, "Sam was offered the horse if he agreed to buy the animal at a stated price. Sam paused and thought he was being taken advantage of. Sam said he would not pay anything for the horse considering he would have significant veterinarian bills to pay and would be investing his time and effort to take care of its broken leg." Jack said, "The owner relented and accepted Sam's offer."

"When traffic finally moved again, the vehicle pulling the horse trailer followed Sam's car to the country home where Sam lived." Jack smiled. "The horse turned out to be a mare. The owner told Sam that the horse's name was Molly. Sam knew a veterinarian whom he called to come and take care of the broken bone. Afterwards Sam carefully followed the instructions given by the vet. I seem to remember hearing the horse wore a cast on her leg for a time. Now, after three months under Sam's care, the horse is doing well. I think the cast over the fracture helped a lot. I don't know all the details, but I sure have heard from Sam how much he loves Molly."

Grandmother Rose added, "I knew he was excited about getting the horse, but what I like is how he laughs now when he talks with me on the phone. Before, he had always seemed so serious—and sort of at a loss for what to talk about."

Amy changed the subject. "The timer just went off in the kitchen. It means our lunch is ready. Let's go enjoy it." The group moved to the dining room where Amy had earlier set out an individual bowl and a tablespoon on the table for each person there. Lunch was a delicious stew served with homemade biscuits and a special fruit drink.

That afternoon seemed to fly by quickly to Sarah. The more she observed Jack, the more she respected him. He was noticing nice things about her as well. She observed his brown hair matched the color of his eyes. He was a head taller than she was. He observed Sarah's curly blonde hair and her blue eyes. Her cute laugh made him smile.

It was when they happened to look directly into each other's eyes during a discussion that changed things between Sarah and Jack. Suddenly to them, it seemed they were the only ones in the room. They each felt a deep satisfying feeling of an internal blending occurring.

The others in the room smiled as they observed what was happening. They were careful not to add any conversation which would interfere with the blending that was taking place between Sarah and Jack.

Jack asked Sarah for her e-mail address. After she gave it to him, Jack said he'd send her an e-mail later. When she received it, she'd have his e-mail address so no need to ask him for it now.

It seemed all too soon to Sarah when it was time for her to go back home. She said goodbye to Grandmother Rose and felt like hugging Jack goodbye, but resisted the temptation. She did hug Amy before leaving the house and heading towards her car parked in the driveway. She was surprised to discover that Jack had followed her.

"I'm glad we met," Jack said. "I want you to know that I'm not married and am not going steady with anyone at the present time. I did have a girlfriend, but she found someone else she liked better. I need to know if you are seriously romantically involved with anyone in which case I will ignore my feelings about you and leave you alone."

Once assured that Sarah was not involved in any romance and truly would like to keep in touch with him, Jack placed his arms around her and kissed her on her lips. He was greatly pleased how Sarah responded. The couple exchanged house addresses and phone numbers which they recorded on their individual cell phones.

It was an hour later when Grandmother Rose became worried that Jack hadn't returned to the house. She wondered if he had fallen or something and needed help.

Amy looked out the front window of the living room. "Yep," she said smiling. "It looks like he did fall---in love, I mean. Both Sarah and him are standing close together with his arms around her. She has the sweetest smile I've ever seen her have."

"That's really nice," Grandmother Rose replied. "I like Sarah. I'm glad you were able to arrange for the two of them to meet."

A bit later when Jack returned into the house, both women noticed a faint lipstick mark just above his upper lip. Winking at her grandmother, Amy asked Jack if he and Sarah had talked more about people with marks on their foreheads. She was really surprised to learn that the subject had come up between them.

Jack said, "Both she and I feel there is life on at least one other planet. She feels the people there are much more scientifically advanced than we Earth inhabitants are. She said she is going to check at the local library to see if she can find a book on the subject. I mentioned maybe there might be something of interest regarding that on the Internet. She said that she would check that too. As we talked about things, I was surprised how our views seem so much alike. We agreed to share with each other what information we discover about flying saucers. And about other things relating to the people from another planet."

Jack paused and then added, "And yes, to learn more about the similar mark on some people's foreheads not far from their noses."

"Hump," replied Grandmother Rose, "That doesn't sound like a very romantic conversation." Jack just smiled in response.

CHAPTER ELEVEN

A few days later, Sarah went to the large public library in her city. She asked the librarian to help locate books about the subjects relating to people who came from outer space and descriptions about their spacecraft. The result was that Sarah checked out a book to take home.

That evening, Sarah phoned Jack and told him about the library book she'd checked out. His response was regret that he didn't have time currently to read books about that. He had some class assignments to complete before they were overdue. He went on to say that his university graduation was scheduled in the upcoming May. It was important to him to graduate with good grades. While chatting on the telephone, Jack paused and then made a date to meet Sarah on the upcoming Saturday afternoon.

In the book Sarah started reading that evening, she discovered a description about how silent the spaceships flew. The author said they came from a planet which was light years away from Earth. These spaceships could fly rapidly or very slowly. They seem to have technology that enabled them to travel extremely long distances in a relatively short period of time. The people aboard the spaceships apparently could breathe the Earth air without wearing face masks. That seemed to indicate their home planet had oxygen like Earth does. The description of the alien's appearance in the book matched that of Grandma's description of them. It indicated the spacemen did not have facial beards. They had dark hair on their heads. The height of most of these alien adults ranged between five feet four inches and five feet eight inches. Both the male and female aliens had broad shoulders and a short neck. They appeared healthy and strong.

That night, Sarah had a dream which seemed ever so real at the time. In the dream, she was on a spaceship. She was being taken to a place where she would be artificially inseminated each year with alien male sperm. She was to be the mother of a child annually for as long as possible. Maybe a way would be found for her to have more than one baby during a pregnancy. She was to be treated exceptionally well during her time on the other planet. It would be like she was a precious royal princess. When she could no longer get pregnant, she would be given the opportunity to return to Earth if she wished, but by then, it was felt doubtful she would want to go back.

After Sarah awoke, she blinked her eyes and thought about the dream that had seemed so real. The thought of being a human "broodmare" for the aliens troubled her deeply. She questioned whether she would really choose not to go back to Earth. She wondered, if it actually happened, would she have had any contact with her children after they were born? Her impression was that she would not. Then, becoming wider awake, she scolded herself. Aloud she whispered, "Don't be silly. It was just a dream."

CHAPTER TWELVE

Saturday came and Jack arrived as had been scheduled for that afternoon. He carried a Bible in his hand. When Sarah stared at it, Jack smiled.

"I remember reading something in The Book of Revelation, the last book of the Bible. If you are willing, I would like to invite you to discuss it with me," Jack answered Sarah's puzzled expression.

"Well, come on into the kitchen and we'll sit by the table. You can place the Bible there where you can easily refer to it," Sarah replied.

Jack sat down and placed his Bible on the table in front of himself. Sarah filled two glasses of water. She placed one beside Jack and the other where she was going to sit facing him.

"It's good to see you again," Sarah said, smiling at Jack. "It is also good that you feel free to talk with me about things in the Bible. It sometimes is difficult to feel free to talk about that with some people. Please tell me what you want to share with me."

"This book in the Bible describes what some people call *the latter days*. This book prophesizes that people will be faced by several challenges, like food costing a lot--a whole lot more-- and that there will be new diseases. There may be one or more events that cause worldwide devastation." Jack was frowning as he said that. He seemed concerned about the predicted coming events.

"We have a new disease called Covid," Sarah sighed. "I wonder if that fits into the prophecy."

"The way I interpret what I read is that this approaching period of many hardships will begin to become especially noticeable in the near future, and that it will last for about three years," Jack said.

"Many people are out of work now," answered Sarah. "I hear that some people in large metropolitan areas already live in tents. Some can't afford the increased monthly house or apartment costs on their salaries. Others have lost their jobs."

"I find it amazing that what seems about to occur in our lifetime was predicted about two thousand years ago in the Bible." Jack smiled. "It gives me a sense of fulfillment somehow. Yes, and that God is actually in control in spite of what the circumstances appear. I wonder if the space people are a part of this plan, and if they will rescue humans with the forehead mark before the calamity strikes."

Sarah chuckled. "Got it all figured out, have you? Like it is in God's plan and, therefore, is not something to be scared about."

Jack replied, "Oh, no. I think it is something to worry about and take precautions to prepare for ahead of time. It is like the prediction was included in the last book of the Bible so people could prepare for the extreme difficult time before it arrived. Still, it is good knowing God is in control no matter how harsh circumstances might seem."

Sarah resolved to later read the last book in the Bible herself and see what is said there about the predicted quickly approaching circumstances. She wanted to come to her own conclusion and then later compare it to Jack's interpretation.

"I'm glad you brought this to my attention, Jack. I would like to read the Scripture you mention in private, pray about it, and ask for divine guidance in understanding the full meaning of it and what, if anything, I should do as result. Let's drop this serious subject until after I read the Bible passages about it."

Jack smiled and nodded his head.

"Would you like to go for a bike ride? I'm sure my brother wouldn't mind if you borrow his bike. I have one of my own," Sarah said as she stood.

Jack smiled, stood, and placed the Bible on the table. He held Sarah's hand as the two left the house and went into the attached garage where the bicycles were stored. It was a warm, but not hot, sunny day, a great time for a bicycle ride.

CHAPTER THIRTEEN

May arrived and Jack graduated from his university with high grades. He was offered a job with a salary far higher than he expected. It was with a company which had an outlet in northern Alaska. If he accepted the offered position there, part of his salary would include a house in which to live. It was adjacent to the place where he would be working.

Jack asked Sarah to marry him and then move with him to the new job in Alaska. Sarah paused. Yes, she loved Jack deeply, but was she willing to move to a place that seemed very isolated and away from all of her friends and relatives? It seemed to her that if she moved to the suggested location, she would be living in a place that was snowed in during late autumn, all of winter, and then part of spring. What other women lived nearby? Would the weather keep her isolated in the house? Where would they buy groceries if they lived there? There were a lot of unanswered questions. What if she got pregnant? Was there a doctor nearby?

Jack watched the various expressions cross the face of his beloved. He noticed her frown.

"I probably could get another job locally, honey. It wouldn't pay nearly the same salary though. There are options we can choose from," Jack said.

Sarah heaved a big sigh of relief. "Jack, I love you deeply. Yes, I want to share my life with you, but I don't want to live in that particular isolated place in Alaska."

Jack smiled. "That settles it. I'll turn the job down, darling. Your happiness is very important to me." The couple started kissing.

It was a week later when Sarah's brother, Chris, asked her if he could look at the notes their grandmother had provided about the flying saucer people. Sarah was happy to share what she had already organized chronologically. She watched her brother's facial expressions as Chris began reading the first page and then continued page after page. After Chris was finished reading the notes, Sarah brought up the discussion she had with Jack about the Bible prophecy.

Chris replied, "Our grandmother sure had a vivid imagination. It seems like she had a dream when she was five years old. Later, when she was bored, it was like she used her imagination to add more to the dream. I think all of what she wrote about Spaceman and those like him is completely hogwash—untrue. I think it gave her a certain sense of satisfaction to write what she did, but it wasn't based upon true facts. And, I don't believe the Bible prophecy about hard times coming to us in the near future."

Sarah frowned. "But, Chris, what if the Bible prophecy IS true? It would indicate that we people now living on Earth are soon going to face some hard times. I wonder if the outer space people are a part of the prophecy, and if they will rescue the chosen ones before the hard times come. I very much doubt that those from outer space would be able to help all of us. It would seem wise to collect a large food supply to offset the shortages and extremely high prices predicted to come in the near future."

Chris studied Sarah's face. "Do you really believe that the Bible prediction is soon to come true? And besides, it was written over two thousand years ago! What makes you think that the many translations that have occurred over the centuries were done accurately? Why do you think that outer space aliens, if they do exist, have any role in saving some Earth people if conditions occur fulfilling the prophecies of the Book of Revelation? It just doesn't make sense to me, Sis."

Sarah sighed. "I don't know why, Chris, but I have an inside feeling that what the Bible predicts will actually occur."

"Sis, I do not believe that the Bible was intended to always be interpreted literally, but rather, with some passages as stories to teach moral lessons. But, understand that I am stating my own opinion. It in no way detracts from your right to your own opinion. I believe that my beliefs do not have to be the same as yours. I do feel that each individual has the right to his or her own religious beliefs, and that we should be tolerant of each other's views. No matter how different our opinions are from one another, you are my sister, and I love you."

Sarah blinked. Then she said, "Thank you for your words, Chris. I love you, too. But, putting the Bible prophecy aside, what about what some people have seen in the sky and which has been reported in newspapers? These spacecrafts were identified in the newspaper articles as possible visitors from another planet."

Chris answered, "It did attract readers, didn't it? And if some nation has secret advanced aircraft, it might not be wise to admit publicly that the observed special flight craft was theirs. Much better to let people believe in flying saucers from another planet. Doesn't that make sense?"

Sarah replied, "That could be. It does sound logical. And yet, my intuition tells me that people from another planet do visit Earth."

"Oh Sis, time will tell which one of us is correct. In the meantime, if nothing changes regarding the reported sightings of this particular type of craft, things will continue to go on as they have. No need to be overly concerned. If a war breaks out, though, between nations here on Earth, I think the country with the most advanced military equipment, including aircraft, will be the winner."

Sarah sighed. "Guess we don't have to fret about the sightings now anyway. The aircraft don't seem to be a threat."

Chris smiled. "Hey, Sis. How about a bowl of ice cream? You and I don't have to worry about what is in the sky from time to time. Let our country's leaders have that responsibility." As he spoke, Chris removed the ice cream container from the freezer and brought it to the kitchen table. Sarah went to the cupboard and removed two bowls. She took a tablespoon and two teaspoons from the drawer under the counter top. Abruptly, the conversation changed to plans each had for the coming weekend.

CHAPTER FOURTEEN

Time seemed to fly to Sarah after she married Jack. The newlyweds moved into an apartment not far from the job Jack had found and liked. Sarah found a job in a local newspaper office as a receptionist. One day when she answered the phone, she heard an excited voice saying he'd seen a flying saucer hovering over Morgan Lake. Could the newspaper send a reporter to take pictures and cover the story? Sarah transferred the call to Mr. Pearson, the newspaper's chief editor. Eagerly, Sarah waited to hear the result.

Mr. Pearson placed a phone call to his star reporter, Steve Adams, who had earned the nickname of "Seek 'Em Steve." Steve could seek and find a story where many others never even suspected was there was one.

When the newspaper reporter came back from the location of the alleged scene where the suspected spaceship was said to have been seen, Sarah was delighted that he had to wait to talk to Mr. Pearson. The reporter sat in a chair not far from where Sarah was on duty. She took advantage of the time to find out what the reporter discovered. At first, he was reluctant to talk about it. Finally, he said, "I thought it was a waste of time until I saw the man, Paul Andrews, who reported the flying saucer sighting. I'd arrived in a car with the name of our newspaper on the front door. Paul immediately came up to me and introduced himself."

"Then what happened?" Sarah asked.

According to Steve, Paul Andrews had seen a spaceship hovering over Morgan Lake and was able to snap a few photos on his cell phone. He became distracted for a moment when a squirrel running down a tree trunk created a strange sounding noise. When Paul turned back to look at the spaceship after seeing the small animal, the spaceship was gone. Had he imagined it? No, it had been real. He looked at the photos on his cell phone. He felt they were worth sharing with others.

Paul showed Steve, the newspaper reporter, the pictures he'd taken on his cell phone. Before Steve left the scene, Paul forwarded to Steve's cell phone the photos of the spaceship.

Much to her delight, Steve offered to show Sarah the pictures. Yes, she thought, that looks like what Grandma had described regarding spaceships from outer space. Aloud, Sarah asked, "Would you mind sharing the pictures of the spaceship with me?"

Steve was pleased that Sarah was so interested. He asked for her cell phone number and forwarded copies of the photos. Just then, Sarah's interoffice phone rang. The chief editor was ready to speak with his star reporter. Steve waved goodbye to Sarah and went smiling to talk to Mr. Pearson.

Sarah was surprised to learn later that Mr. Pearson had decided not to have the pictures or the story published his daily newspaper. He felt it would just be what he called "an old hat" article if it were printed. "There are similar stories already in the public mind, including various pictures of what the spaceships are said to look like. There is no way to prove these pictures shown to me today are really true ones. I have the feeling Mr. Andrews was expecting a cash reward for a story he had invented, and he likely created the pictures using artificial intelligence."

Sarah did not expect Mr. Pearson's reaction, but she understood it. Sarah kept her opinion to herself, but she wondered silently if Mr. Andrews would try to have the story published in another newspaper.

Amy stopped by Sarah's house the following evening. Sarah could hardly wait to show Amy the pictures of the spacecraft Steve had shared with her. These pictures fit the description of the spacecraft as described in Grandma Alexia's notes. Sarah was convinced that the story told by Paul to Steve was authentic.

As Amy carefully studied one of the photos that Sarah was displaying on the computer monitor, she said, "It is hard to prove this is an authentic picture. It might be a reproduction of some earlier picture that this Paul guy copied, or it could have been created by using artificial intelligence."

"Maybe," replied Sarah, "but I truly believe that Paul was telling the truth, and the pictures are authentic ones he snapped on his cell phone."

"Sometimes, dear Sarah, it is easy to believe what we want to be true," replied Amy. "It sounds like this Paul was very convincing in what he told Steve. Liars can make things sound truthful."

Sarah felt really stunned and inwardly wounded about Amy's remarks. Aloud she replied, "Okay, lets drop the subject. Tell me about your new boyfriend."

The next weekend, Sarah was pleased when she received a phone call from the reporter, Steve Adams. She listened as he excitedly told her that he found a publisher who wanted him and Paul Andrews to write a book titled *Flying Saucer Spotted*. Steve wondered if Sarah would be interested in adding information to it regarding her grandmother's notes. Steve reminded her that she had mentioned her grandmother's notes when he'd showed her the pictures of the spacecraft hovering over the lake.

Sarah felt stunned. "I—I don't know what to say," she answered. "How would we go about working on it together?"

"You could e-mail me copies of your notes. We could work out the details. I'd be sure to add your name as a third co-author with Paul and me and equally share any profit the publication produces." Paul had previously given Steve permission to work out the initial co-author details with Sarah.

Sarah paused and then said, "Could you come and talk with me and my husband—or we could meet you someplace?"

Steve replied, "Give me your address and tell me when would be a good time for me to arrive. It would be a great thing to do this project together. I would like to share our knowledge with others regarding visitors from another planet." Sarah sensed that Steve was excited about the book project. He felt her contributions would make the book more complete.

A date and time were set for Steve to come to the home of Sarah and Jack. Sarah was given Steve's phone number.

When she told Jack about the phone call, he looked doubtful. "Can you trust this man to use correctly whatever information you give him, sweetheart? Would it be used in a constructive way? How well do you know this person? Can you completely trust him?"

Sarah paused. She'd only talked face to face with Steve for a short time while he was in the office waiting room. She didn't really know the man. Yet, intuitively she felt he was trustworthy. Finally, she replied, "Let's talk with him when he comes here. We could create a written contract with Steve and Paul to protect our interests if we submit material for this book. You could make the final decision about whether we work with him or not."

CHAPTER FIFTEEN

Steve arrived by 2 PM Saturday afternoon as had been arranged during the recent phone call. Jack studied the guest. Steve and Jack asked questions of each other. Somehow, a feeling of respect and trust was being established between the two men.

Gradually, it became evident to Sarah that Jack liked and trusted Steve. Steve felt similar feelings towards Jack. Sarah knew they had all become a team to get information into a book about alien spacecraft and their occupants. The next thing was to decide how to go about this endeavor. Paul would need to be included in future meetings.

"Are we going to include opinions and information from others who have actually seen flying saucers from outer space?" Sarah asked. "Or, is the book to contain just about what my grandmother wrote in her notes and what you and Paul can add, Steve? And Jack, should we ask your brother, Sam, if he would like to contribute to the book, since he saw a flying saucer?"

Steve turned towards his new friend, Jack, as he said "I'm of the opinion we should restrict our book to just Sarah's grandmother's notes and opinions, and add details and pictures of the spacecraft from Paul. What do you think, Jack?"

Sarah smiled to herself as she watched the various expressions on her husband's face. He was frowning as he inwardly debated the question and its answers. Finally, Jack sighed and said, "I think we should restrict the book to the things we personally experienced and know and those that were written by Grandma Alexia. I think we should not ask Sam, since his sighting led to the trauma of being bullied in school, and he wants to forget about it."

Sarah added, "I agree with that. We are all in agreement about this. So, how do we start the book? How is the reader to be introduced to the subject?"

"Hold on---Let's not worry about some things until later. The big thing is how to interest a reader to want to continue reading it once the first few pages are read," Jack said.

It took Sarah, Steve, and Paul working together for several weeks to have the final contents of the book satisfactory to each of the three of its authors.

The three authors and Jack met to discuss more details about the book, including how the book's proceeds would be distributed. Paul said that he would like to donate part of his share of the proceeds to his favorite charity.

Steve had a similar idea, and said, "Now that we are ready to have the book published, I would be gratified if I could have some of my share of the proceeds donated to my favorite charity that helps so many people." He smiled as he mentioned the charity's name.

"Oh my, that's was my grandmother's favorite charity too." Sarah paused. "If still alive, I believe she would have been happy if some of the proceeds from the book were donated there as well." Turning towards her husband, she added, "But do we want to do that?"

Jack paused and then smiled. "We are going to use much of what Grandma provided in this book, and she will be given credit for the information that she contributed. I'd be happy if a portion of the proceeds is donated to her favorite charity. But what are your thoughts, honey?" He studied his wife's facial expressions.

Sarah said nothing for a moment. Then smiling, she replied. "I agree with you, and I can imagine what Grandma's reaction would have been if she knew her effort to save her information was eventually going to be used in this way." Sarah gave Jack a big hug. "Yes, let's agree to donate a percentage of the gross proceeds to charity, pay any expenses, and then divide the remainder evenly between the three authors. We'll figure out the exact percentage to donate to charity later."

Steve sighed. "Well, that was an easy solution about what to do with the proceeds if there are any. Now, let's get busy and get the book ready for publication."

After the book was published, reader response was slow at first, but later it was added to a Suggested Readers' List in a popular magazine. The book created an interest among many people regarding alien beings and other planets.

Steve, Paul, Sarah and Jack were delighted when they discovered a new subject was soon to be introduced in the local college about the latest information regarding planets in the universe and if any of them could support human life. The class would include likely human survival challenges on these other planets. Added to the curriculum would be information on the advancements in human space travel and the expectation that further improvements would be developed in the future.

A few months after the book was published, Sarah was mesmerized by a giant unnaturally beautiful butterfly in her garden. She was so focused on the butterfly that complete silence seemed to surround her. Sarah sensed an alien presence standing behind her. The butterfly faded away.

Esther R. Smith

The Earth Visitor and Alexia

Other books by this author:

(Available from Amazon.com)

Surviving 1930 to 1946, The Great Depression and Civilian Life During and After World War II

A Memoir by Esther R. Smith

This book recounts the author's memories of growing up in California during the Great Depression and civilian life during the turbulent times of World War II. This book covers the years 1930 through 1946. By 1946, people's outlook had brightened considerably. The author's father lost his job while the severe financial depression was fully under way, and it was a long time before he found a new one. Expenses don't stop just because a paycheck has. The author's family was not alone in facing unemployment; nearly 30% of the work force in California lost their jobs. Times were very hard. Civilian life after the United States entered World War II was a time of shortages, price controls and civilian rationing of gasoline, meat, and other items. Fear of possible invasion by enemy forces was a subtle worry. Men up to age 35 were subject to being drafted into military service. Sadness caused by war casualties was also part of civilian life.

Two Kingdoms

by Esther Thomson Smith

It was a bit windy, but Prince Melvin decided to take his two cousins for a hot air balloon ride as he had promised to do on the day after he earned his pilot's license to operate one. A fatal mishap ended the lives of all in the balloon's basket. Was it an accident or a skillfully committed assassination? After watching the balloon start to lift into the air, Vernetta, the sixteen- year-old sister of

Melvin, and her nineteen-year-old second cousin, Prince Jacob, sneaked to a tattoo shop for a hidden permanent symbol of their love and promise to marry when Vernetta turned twenty-one, the accepted marriage age for a princess of her country. King Elphonsio of North Nolaland, Vernetta's father, did not know of these secret marriage plans. He accepted a huge bribe to pledge Vernetta would marry King Zerlone of the large neighboring country of Kolten. Vernetta was shocked when she heard the news. King Zerlone already had three former wives all of whom died while pregnant. And she, Vernetta was expected to be the fourth wife? Two of the countries of Zerlone's former wives had been absorbed into Kolten. Was this going to happen to North Nolaland? In the legend that Vernetta heard as a child and believed, a powerful fairy named Nola was the guardian of Nolaland. Years before, the legend said, Nola had been called away from her beloved area, but she had promised she would return if she was ever needed. Was now that time?

Broken Engagement - Joan's Story

by Esther Thomson Smith

Nineteen-year-old Joan Alexander never felt happier. Last night her beloved Richard Seymour slipped an engagement ring on her finger. She is blissfully unaware that her dreams of a wonderful future with Richard are about to be torn apart and shattered. This Tuesday morning Joan is a little late leaving home to go to her university class, but she never arrives. She is kidnapped by a man disguised with a wig of long black hair and a false bushy beard of the same color. He takes her to an isolated cabin. He says it doesn't have to be his right name, but she can call him Mike. He tells Joan that he has been hired by a mystery woman whom he gives the code name of Black Crow. In order to stay alive, Joan must do as Black Crow demands. The first thing required by Black Crow is for Joan to write a letter to Richard breaking their engagement and returning his ring. What is going to happen next? Why is Mike so interested in keeping Black Crow appeased in order to keep Joan safe? Why is it so important to him that Joan's mother had red hair?

Made in United States
Troutdale, OR
12/20/2024

27051855R00076